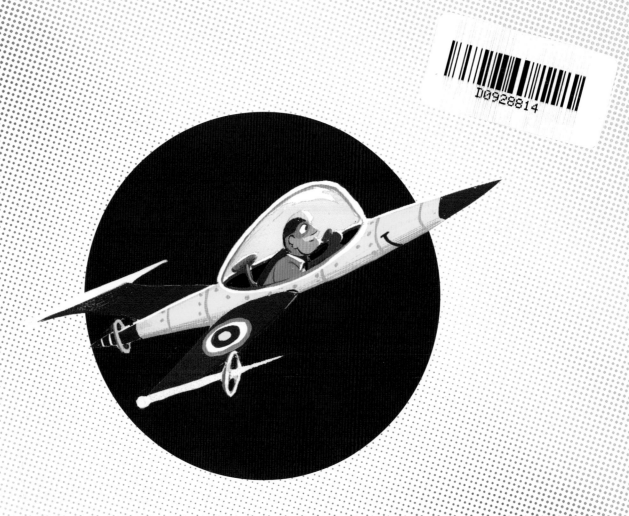

Ice Woman

Mr Invisible

Gadget Girl

RECEPTION

Joe Maloe

The Flame

Captain Power

Superhero HOTEL

Abie Longstaff

Migy Blanco

SCHOLASTIC

Above the **cliff**,

through the **meadow**,

past the **rocks**,

over the **lake**,

at the top of the **hill**

stood a secret hotel.

This was the **Superhero Hotel**, the place where superheroes came to relax, and **Joe Maloe** looked after every single one.

One morning, **Captain Power** stumbled into reception.

"I had to stop a runaway train," he puffed, "It took all my **Super Strength**."

"I'll put you in the **Recharge Room**," said Joe Maloe.

At lunchtime, in came **Gadget Girl**.
All her tools were covered in mud.

"A cave fell in," she said.
"I needed my **Mega Grabber**
to rescue everyone."

"I'll wash your tools," said Joe Maloe,
and he led Gadget Girl to the **Turbo-Cleaning Room**.

Then came **Ice Woman** with a frozen splinter stuck in her thumb,

The Flame, whose **Blaze Boots** needed new fire-proof heels,

and finally **Mr Invisible**,

although nobody saw him but Joe.

For the next few days everybody rested.

The Superhero Hotel was quiet
– except for the sound of
Captain Power snoring.

Soon everyone was better. In fact, they all felt **so** much better they started to get...

"Just **rest**," said Joe Maloe. "Everything's fine.
I'll be doing some work on the garden if you need me."

"**We'll help!**" the superheroes cried.
They rushed into the garden.

Mr Invisible came too,
although nobody saw him but Joe.

At **first**, everything was peaceful.

Captain Power lifted trees in his strong arms so Joe could reach the weeds underneath.

The Flame decided to build a barbecue in the garden.

Ice Woman thought the outdoor swimming pool might be better used as a skating rink.

And Gadget Girl started building a rocket to make the hotel lift move at supersonic speed — up and down, side to side, into the garden and back.

But then...

Captain Power stepped backwards and **tripped** over Mr Invisible.

"**Whoah!**" he wibbled and wobbled.

The Flame was just about to shoot a firebolt to light her new barbecue when she was **bumped** by Captain Power.

The firebolt **shot** past
Gadget Girl and straight to...

FIZZ
went the fuse.

the fuse of her rocket.

HOOSH!

BANG!

The rocket
took off...

...and *skidded* across the ice.

SWOOOOSH!

The rocket **smashed** into the hotel...

KAPOW!

and it **shot** forward to the edge of the hill!

With **lightning fast** speed the superheroes leapt onto the hotel roof.

"We'll save the hotel!" they cried.

Down the hill the hotel sped, faster and *faster!*

It was headed straight for the lake.

The superheroes looked at each other.

Who was the right hero for the job?

They **zoomed** across the meadow at top speed.

Faster and **faster** they went.

We need to **STOP** that rocket!

the superheroes cried.

And **THEN...**

Mr Invisible put out the rocket fire with a bucket of water.

Although nobody saw him but Joe.

The hotel came to
a **screeching** stop.

It **teetered** at the
very edge of the cliff.

"Everyone off!"
shouted Gadget Girl,
"I know what to do."

She **shot** her **Mega Grabber**, looping it round the chimney.

Then Captain Power **pulled**

the hotel from danger

with his **Super Strength**.

Everyone cheered.

HURRAY

"Thank you all for saving the hotel,"
said Joe Maloe.

The superheroes were very tired.

"Everybody rest," said Joe. "It's **my** turn to help. My **super power** is: I know how to look after all of you."

A little *too* high.

"*Hurray for Joe Maloe!*"
called Gadget Girl, and
Captain Power **threw** him
high into the air.

Luckily Mr Invisible was on hand to catch him...

...although nobody saw him but Joe.

For K&E

A.L.

For the three
superheroes in my life

M.B.

First published in 2017 by Scholastic Children's Books
Euston House, 24 Eversholt Street
London NW1 1DB
a division of Scholastic Ltd
www.scholastic.co.uk
London ~ New York ~ Toronto ~ Sydney ~ Auckland
Mexico City ~ New Delhi ~ Hong Kong

Text copyright © 2017 Abie Longstaff
Illustrations copyright © 2017 Migy Blanco

PB ISBN 978 1407 16690 2